I HERO

MONSTER HUNTER

DEMON

STEVE BARLOW AND STEVE SKIDMORE

ILLUSTRATED BY PAUL DAVIDSON

Franklin Watts
First published in Great Britain in 2020
by The Watts Publishing Group

ISBN: 978 1 4451 6994 1
ebook ISBN: 978 1 4451 6995 8
Library ebook ISBN: 978 1 4451 6996 5

1 3 5 7 9 10 8 6 4 2

Printed in Great Britain

Franklin Watts
An imprint of
Hachette Children's Group
Part of The Watts Publishing Group
Carmelite House
50 Victoria Embankment
London EC4Y 0DZ

An Hachette UK Company
www.hachette.co.uk

www.hachettechildrens.co.uk

Mission Statement

You are the hero of this mission.

Each section of this book is numbered. At the end of most sections, you will have to make a choice. The choice you make will take you to a different section of the book.

Some of your choices will help you to complete the adventure successfully. But if you make the wrong choice, death may be the best you can hope for! Because even dying is better than being UNDEAD and becoming a slave of the monsters you have sworn to destroy!

Dare you go up against a world of monsters?

All right, then.

Let's see what you've got...

Introduction

You are an agent of **G.H.O.S.T.** — Global Headquarters Opposing Supernatural Threats.

Our world is under constant attack from supernatural horrors that lurk in the shadows. It's your job to make sure they stay there.

You have studied all kinds of monsters, and know their habits and behaviour. You are an expert in disguise, able to move among monsters in human form as a spy. You are expert in all forms of martial arts. G.H.O.S.T. has supplied you with weapons, equipment and other assets that make you capable of destroying any supernatural creature.

G.H.O.S.T.

You are based at Arcane Hall, a spooky and secret-laden mansion. Your butler, Cranberry, is another G.H.O.S.T. agent who assists you in all your adventures, providing you with information and backup.

Your life at Arcane Hall is comfortable and peaceful; but you know that at any moment, the G.H.O.S.T. High Command can order you into action in any part of the world...

Go to 1.

1

You are in India on a well-earned break from saving the world (again). You're visiting the world-famous Taj Mahal, built at the command of the emperor Shah Jahan in the 17th century to house the tomb of his wife.

Wandering around the gardens that surround the marble building, you observe a troop of macaque monkeys in the trees.

A local tour guide sees you admiring the creatures. "The monkeys look lovely, but my advice is to stay clear of them, they can be vicious!"

You think about all the supernatural creatures you have had to face in your career. "Thanks for the warning," you laugh. "But they're only monkeys!"

As you walk towards the tree, the monkeys drop down from the branches and head towards you. You are shocked to see them transforming! Their eyes burn red and their teeth grow into huge, razor-sharp fangs. You realise what they are. They aren't 'only monkeys'; they are demon monkeys!

As the Taj Mahal is supposed to be a peaceful place, you didn't bother bringing your weapons with you; they're in your car...

To use your martial arts skills against the monkeys, go to 36.

To run to your car for the weapons, go to 17.

You reach the bridge and step onto the wooden slats. The bridge sways with your every movement.

"Begone, stranger!"

You look ahead and see the shimmering figure of a demon warrior blocking your way. The creature holds a kaman bow and notches an arrow into its drawstring.

"Begone, stranger!"

"OK, there's no need to repeat yourself. I get your message," you say.

To use your flame pistol, go to 23.
To use your BAM gun, go to 34.

3

You drop through the clouds, concentrating on your altimeter.

500 metres... 400 metres... 300 metres...

You reach 250 metres and wait for the auto-chute device to kick in. Nothing happens!

200 metres...

The experimental auto-deploy device has failed!

100 metres...

You manually deploy your spare chute. It begins to open, but you've left it too late! You smash into the forest!

Hitting the ground at that speed? There's only one winner and it's not you! Go back to 1.

4

You take out the amulet and hold it up. "Okay, amulet, do whatever magic stuff you're supposed to do," you mutter.

Nothing happens.

"I'm waiting!" you cry.

Mouth open, the cobra's head suddenly jerks downwards. You feel its fangs pierce your skin and pain shoots through your body. The snake's venom pumps through your veins and you pass out.

Why did you trust in a jewel you just happened to find? Go back to 1.

5

Sometime later, you arrive at an abandoned village. Troops of monkeys and exotic, colourful birds inhabit the surrounding trees. You move through the ruined huts, searching for any signs of life.

On the floor in one of the huts you see an amber-coloured amulet. You pick it up and examine a series of strange symbols scratched into its surface.

I'll get Cranberry to check these out, when I make contact, you think and put it in your bag.

Finding nothing else, you head back to the path. As you pass out of the village, a racket of

noise breaks out from the trees. The birds are
shrieking and the monkeys screaming.

Then the noise suddenly stops.

To investigate the situation, go to 49.
To get the heck out of there, go to 37.

6

"There's no time to waste, so let's get going," you say to Cranberry.

"Your enthusiasm is to be applauded, Agent, but you need to know a bit more about the mission," says Cranberry. "An uninformed agent usually becomes a dead agent!"

You realise that Cranberry is right.

Go to 24.

7

"Interesting story," you say, "but let's see if you're telling the truth."

You take out the TAME flute and begin to play. The Raja looks on quizzically as nothing happens...

"Okay, so you haven't transformed into what you really are, so by remaining in the same state, you really are who you say you are and your story is true! If you get my drift..."

The Raja looks solemn. "If you do not trust me, I think I would be unwise to trust you and so I cannot share my knowledge with you."

You wonder what this knowledge could be...

The Raja continues, "Thank you for freeing me from this spell of enchantment, but I must ask you to leave."

Go to 25.

8

You pull out your BAM gun and begin to blast at the oncoming bats. They are no match for the firepower of your weapon and soon the sky is clear of the demon creatures.

You land in the forest and check your coordinates. The bat fight has made you land some distance away from the temple. You try your comms link, but can't get through to Cranberry.

To send up a drone, go to 26.
To set off to the tomb, go to 31.

9

You decide to take the tunnel that glows green.

As you make your way through the tunnel, there's a roaring noise and the ground beneath your feet gives way.

Go to 38.

10

"How did you do that?" you ask.

Cranberry holds up the flute. "It's a TAME weapon. It Tames All Monsters Easily. The sound is set at a certain pitch, which vibrates the DNA of any monster that has changed form. It transforms the creature into what it was before. Rather good, isn't it?"

"But what are you doing here?" you ask.

"Apart from saving your backside, I was sent by the Director General to investigate sightings of demon activity in India."

"Why didn't she give me the mission?" you ask.

"I believe she wanted you to have a rest from saving the world!"

To continue your holiday, go to 21.
To take on the mission, go to 42.

11

You take out your BAM gun as the warriors stomp towards you, swords raised.

Clambering up one of the marble walls you begin shooting. The warriors are slow, so you keep moving, running around the walls of the palace, leaping over ledges and keeping out of reach.

You take out the warriors one by one and soon there is nothing left of your enemies but piles of rubble littering the palace courtyard.

As you clamber down from the walls, you hear the music still coming from inside the palace.

To investigate the music, go to 20.
To continue on your journey, go to 25.

12

You reach into your bag for the TAME flute and begin to play. But the bats are not close enough and the wind carries the sounds away from the demon creatures!

To reach for the BAM gun, go to 8.
To steer away from the bats, go to 19.

13

You begin firing at the creatures.

But while you are dealing with these enemies, a group of blue-skinned demons moves forward. Each has ten arms and each pair of arms holds a drawn bow. That's five bows each, aimed at you.

Before you can shoot at them, they release their arrows. Pain rips through your body and you drop to the floor. It's the end of the adventure for you.

Have you got the point? Don't take on too many demons at once! Go back to 1.

14

"Parachute, of course. It'll be quicker," you tell Cranberry. "Let's go..."

Soon you are flying south in the Phantom Flyer. "Tell me what we know about this Demon King, Cranberry," you say.

"We believe this Demon King is building up his forces across India by calling upon the spirits of the underworld. We don't know what his ultimate goal is."

You shake your head. "I'd bet it's world domination and bringing misery to all mankind. Supernatural forces don't do peace and love."

As Cranberry pilots the flyer, you load your weapons bag with a BAM (Blasts All Monsters) gun and flame pistol. You also take the TAME weapon.

As you approach the drop, the weather turns wretched. Black clouds stretch out across the sky and thunder and lightning rock the flyer.

"This will make parachuting almost impossible. I advise going to the airport," says Cranberry.

To take Cranberry's advice, go to 45.
To ignore it, go to 33.

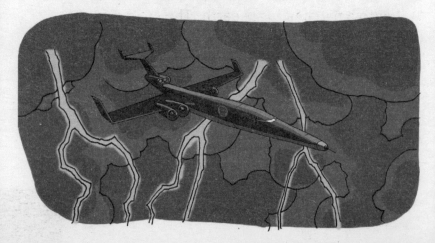

15

You decide it would be best to take the safe route until you can re-establish a link to Cranberry, so you follow an old forest track.

Several hours later your comms link lights up. It's Cranberry! "Where are you?" you ask.

"I'm afraid I'm being sent home and so are you Agent — the DG is not happy about us taking so long. The Demon King has unleashed his warriors on the world and it's too late to stop him!"

Taking the safe option? What sort of agent are you? Go back to 1.

16

You hack at the undergrowth, but still can't see any sign of the temple.

As you continue to search the area, you step onto a patch of loose earth. The ground gives way beneath your feet and you find yourself falling downwards.

Go to 38.

17

You turn and run from the creatures, but there are hundreds of screaming tourists in your way. Desperately you try to get through the fleeing crowd.

"Let me through! I'm in pest control!" you shout. But there are too many people to push through and the monkeys are catching you.

To continue to try to reach your car, go to 28.

To fight the monkeys, go to 36.

18

The Raja's words spring to mind: *If you wish to encounter the Demon King, you must avoid the colour of jealousy.*

You know that green is the colour of jealousy, so you take the red glowing tunnel and hurry down it — it's time to meet the Demon King once and for all.

Soon you are standing on a rock ledge, looking down into a vast cavern, lit by a lake of lava. A beautiful temple sits in the middle of the lake.

Carved figures of humans, demons, animals and birds cover its walls.

If you wish to send up the drone, go to 30.
If you wish to head down to the temple immediately, go to 46.

19

You pull on your chute's strings to try to steer away from the little beasts, but you are only delaying the inevitable! The cloud of demon bats hits you full on. Their teeth rip at your flesh and you pass into oblivion.

Looks like you were a bat meal deal.
Go back to 1.

20

You move into the palace and observe a young man plucking at the strings of a santoor. He sees you and stops playing. Two tigers lie at his feet. They stare at you with their amber eyes.

The young man speaks. "Welcome! I assume that by being here, you have conquered the demons and so I give you thanks."

"Who are you?" you ask.

"I am the Raja of this state. I was entrapped here many years ago by a Demon King who wished me and my people to follow its ways. I refused and was banished to this magical palace. But now it seems that you have defeated his guards and freed me."

If you trust what the young man is saying, go to 32.

If you don't, go to 7.

21

"Fair enough," you say. "If she doesn't want me, then I'll carry on taking my holiday." You head off. Leaving Cranberry to deal with the demons.

Later that day you get a call from the Director General. "I'm afraid you failed your test, Agent. I wanted to see if you were committed to G.H.O.S.T. It seems that you'd rather take a holiday than deal with supernatural problems. Don't bother coming back. You're fired!"

There's no place for slackers in G.H.O.S.T. Go back to 1.

22

You realise that there are too many enemies to deal with, so you stand still.

The drums begin to sound again as a red-skinned demon emerges onto the steps of the temple. The Demon King raises an arm and the drums cease.

"So the hunter has come to my domain," rasps the demon.

"As I was passing, I thought I'd drop in and say hello," you reply.

The Demon King scowls. "Your 'humour' is known amongst us creatures of the shadows. But you are too late to stop me. The humans who found my temple awoke me. Since that day, I have sent my followers into your world to test whether you will be able to oppose me and you cannot. Now my full powers are ready to be unleashed on your world."

"I told Cranberry it would be the old world domination and bringing misery to all mankind story!" you say.

"Enough of your talk," growls the King. "Bring him to me!" His followers move towards you.

To use the BAM gun, go to 13.
To try to escape, go to 35.
To use the TAME flute, go to 41.

23

You pull the trigger. A stream of flame shoots out engulfing the demon warrior.

"Begone, stranger!" The warrior is unaffected by the flames!

You quickly realise that you've made a big mistake. The only thing you've set alight are the dry ropes and wooden slats of the bridge! It's going to burn away very soon!

To use your BAM gun against the warrior, go to 40.

To dive into the river, go to 47.

"OK, tell me more about the source of the outbreak," you say.

"We've located it to a forest area, north-west of the Jog Falls," replies Cranberry. "There are many ancient tombs and temples in that area. It seems that a group of tomb robbers found a temple and discovered something that disagreed with them. So much so that only one of the robbers made it back alive. He spoke of a Demon King emerging from this temple before he too dropped dead! Ever since then, demon activity has been growing."

"Tomb robbers," you say. "Don't they ever learn? You know something bad will always happen when you mess with ancient tombs and temples! So where is this Jog Falls?"

Cranberry reaches into his 'snake' basket, pulls out a tablet and brings up a map.

"It's too far to drive," you say. "We'll take the Phantom Flyer."

"Do you want to parachute into the forest or land at a nearby airport and pick up a Spook Truck?" asks Cranberry.

To parachute in, go to 14.
To land at a nearby airport, go to 45.

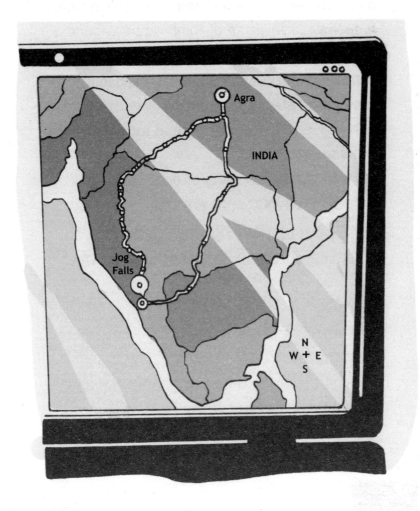

25

You hurry away from the palace and try your comms link. Again, the signal fails to connect. *How am I supposed to save the world when I can't contact anyone!* you think. You try the link again, but it is useless. You decide to continue on your way.

After several hours of hard travelling through dense jungle, you finally arrive at the coordinates of the temple given to you by G.H.O.S.T. HQ. You look around for the temple but see nothing.

"Why do hidden temples have to be so well hidden?" you mutter to yourself.

To send up the drone, go to 44.
To search the undergrowth, go to 16.

26

You send up a drone to spy out the best route to the temple.

Soon the drone is hovering above the jungle, helping you to work out the route you should take.

Within minutes, the drone transmits the information to your comms unit. It gives you two possible routes. You realise that one of the routes is quick and dangerous, whilst the other route will take a lot longer but be considerably safer.

To take the dangerous route, go to 43.
To take the safe one, go to 15.

You scramble across the floor and grab hold of the BAM weapon. As the snake moves in for the kill, you spin around and pull the trigger.

It's a direct hit! The snake thrashes in pain and you fire again. The creature drops to the floor, lifeless.

But you have no time to celebrate as the cavern begins to shake. The temple walls start to crumble and blocks of rock crash around you. You race across the bridge before it is consumed by the boiling lava.

Desperately, you scramble up the cliff as the temple crashes into the lake, sending molten lava high into the air. Sprinting through the collapsing

tunnel you see a glint of daylight ahead and dive through the opening.

You lie panting on the ground and hear a familiar voice. "Agent! I've been looking for you."

Go to 50.

28

You sprint towards the exit, but you're too slow. One of the monkeys smashes into your back and you stumble to the ground.

The other demon monkeys leap on you and rip at your body with their fangs.

Thankfully, the pain fades as you black out.

Stop monkeying around! Go back to 1.

29

You climb down the cliff and reach the river bank. You try to contact Cranberry again, but the link is still down.

Go to 47.

30

You send out the drone to check the area. As you manoeuvre it towards the temple, the air is filled with small darts that shoot out from the cavern walls.

The missiles hit the drone and it drops into the lava.

You're going to have to go in blind!

Go to 46.

31

You set off through the forest, doing your best to follow the coordinates for the tomb. But the way is hard and it takes some time before you reach the banks of a wide river.

This must lead to the Jog Falls, you think.

You look for a crossing point, but there isn't one.

To send up a drone, go to 26.
To swim across the river, go to 47.

32

"Then I am happy to have helped you," you say.

"What brings you to my country?" he asks. You tell him.

"It sounds as though the demon who entrapped me wishes ill on all mankind. Before you go, listen to my words: if you wish to encounter the Demon King, you must avoid the colour of jealousy."

You wonder what the Raja means. "Thank you. I must leave and continue my quest."

Go to 25.

33

"Almost impossible isn't impossible, Cranberry."

"Well don't leave it too late to deploy the parachute," warns Cranberry. "There's an experimental auto-chute device you can use. Set it when you leap out."

You enter the safe-ejection chamber, switch on your comms link and set coordinates for the tomb. "OK, Cranberry, get to the Spook Truck and meet me ASAP!"

The light turns green and you hit eject. You're shot out into the black clouds and hurtle downwards, buffeted by the winds and lightning bolts crashing around you.

To set to auto-open the parachute at 250 metres, go to 3.

To set to auto-open at 500 metres, go to 39.

34

Before the demon warrior can shoot his arrow, you take out your BAM gun and pull the trigger. The creature disappears in a puff of smoke and you make your way across the bridge.

Go to 5.

35

You turn and run. The noise of drumming resumes as the demons race after you.

You reach the cavern wall and try to climb up, but the creatures are right behind you and they pull you to the floor. A demon takes you in its arms, holds you aloft and walks towards the lake. The howls and cackles of the other demons echo around the cavern. You struggle to break free but the creature is too strong. It hurls you into the bubbling lava. Thankfully your pain only lasts seconds.

That was too hot for you to handle! Go back to 1.

All around are screaming tourists, fleeing from the demon creatures.

You turn and face the monkeys. "Right, you lot, no more monkeying around!"

As the demons attack, you grab the tail of one of the creatures. You swing it around and around your head before letting it go. It crashes into its fellow attackers, sending them flying like skittles.

The guide who warned you about the monkeys sees this.

"It's illegal to hurt wild animals in India," he shouts.

"These are more than wild, they're *furious*!" you shout and throw another demon to the ground. But there are too many to deal with. They start to attack the other tourists...

To go to your car to get your weapons, go to 28.

To draw the demons away from the tourists, go to 48.

37

Without looking back, you break into a run.

There is a roar of wind and the air is filled with a rainbow of colours as hundreds of birds swarm all over you, pecking at your face and arms. You are forced to the ground.

You look up into the burning eyes of a demon warrior standing over you. It raises its talwar sword and thrusts it into your body. As your life ebbs away, the birds begin to feast.

Run away? The birds got you, you chicken! Go back to 1.

38

You plunge down and your weapons bag goes flying as you crash against the roots sticking out of the earth walls of the shaft.

You smash into the hard ground and pain rips through your body. You try to raise yourself, but you can't. Your legs are broken. You reach into your pocket and pull out a glowstick.

You gasp in horror as the light reveals hundreds of giant red scorpions. You lie, helpless, as the creatures move towards you, tails raised and venomous stingers ready to strike...

There's a sting in this tale! Go back to 1.

You drop through the clouds, concentrating
on your altimeter. You reach 500 metres and
wait for the auto-chute device to kick in.
Nothing happens!

400 metres...

The experimental auto-deploy device
has failed!

300 metres...

You deploy your spare chute. It opens up and
slows down your descent. *Lucky I didn't leave it
until 250 metres*, you think, *it would have been
pizza time!*

As you drift towards the ground a black cloud
rises up from the trees, heading towards you. You
call up Cranberry. "Have you got a visual
on this?"

"Indeed I have, Agent. It seems a swarm of
demon vampire bats are heading your way!"

To reach for the BAM gun, go to 8.
To reach for the TAME weapon, go to 12.
To steer away from the bats, go to 19.

40

You swap the flame pistol for your BAM gun, but you are too slow.

As the flames engulf the bridge, the warrior shoots an arrow. It pierces your chest and is soon followed by several more.

"Begone, stranger!" are the last words you hear as you plummet down into the raging torrent.

That was some mistake to make!
Go back to 1.

41

You quickly reach into your bag and take out the TAME flute.

"What good will playing a tune do?" mocks the King.

"Let's find out," you reply and you begin to play. The music echoes around the cavern.

Slowly the figures moving towards you grind to a halt as they begin to revert back into what they truly are — stone carvings! Within seconds nothing is moving except the Demon King. As you continue to play, he begins to revert to what he really is — a giant king cobra!

I wasn't expecting that, you think. *You were a snake in the grass all the time!*

The cobra slithers down the steps towards you, mouth open, revealing a set of razor-sharp fangs.

You point your BAM gun, but before you can pull the trigger, the snake's tail whips round and knocks it from your grasp. It clatters across the stone floor.

To use the amulet you picked up, go to 4.
To try to pick up the BAM weapon, go to 27.

"Supernatural forces don't take holidays and neither should a G.H.O.S.T. agent, not when the world's in danger," you say.

"The DG will be happy to hear that," replies Cranberry.

"So what's this demon problem all about?"

"There have been reports of low-level demon activity across India. Our local agents have dealt with these, but now our sources have pinpointed the outbreak to a location in the state of Karnataka."

To get on with the mission, go to 6.
To find out more about the outbreak, go to 24.

43

You decide that there's no time to waste and set off on the quickest route. You hack your way through dense forest vegetation and avoid the poisonous snakes and insects that threaten to end your life.

After a couple of hours of back-breaking effort, you find yourself on the edge of a deep and wide gorge. Below you a river rages. You see a rope and wooden bridge a few hundred metres up the gorge. You take out your vision goggles and zoom in on it. The bridge is in a bad state: wooden slats are missing and the rope is threadbare.

To cross the bridge, go to 2.
To climb down the cliff and swim across the river, go to 29.

You send a drone up and switch to thermal imaging. Seconds later the comms link flashes and you see a heat spot near a small rock face some 50 metres away. *Interesting*, you think, and bring the drone back.

Moving towards the rock face, you take out a machete and hack at the vegetation to reveal a small fissure in the rock. Shining a powerful torch, you look through the opening to see a tunnel.

That's why the temple's been hidden for so long, you think. *It's underground!*

You squeeze through the small opening into the tunnel and move along it. It is dusty and hot and you break into a sweat. Eventually you come to a junction with two tunnels lit by burning torches.

One tunnel glows red and one glows green.

If you met the Raja earlier and he gave you words of advice, go to 18.

If he didn't, go to 9.

45

You decide to head to Hubli airport, some 200 km away from the location of the outbreak.

You land the Phantom Flyer, head for the waiting Spook Truck and set off. You've been travelling for an hour, when the DG contacts you.

"You've taken too long," she says. "There are thousands of demons appearing all over India. We've lost!"

Good agents get on with the job straight away! Go back to 1.

You climb down the cavern wall and step onto the stone bridge leading to the temple. As you do so, the cavern is filled with the deafening noise of beating drums. The lake erupts, sending spouts of boiling-hot lava into the air.

Avoiding the deadly streams, you take out your BAM gun and continue to move across the bridge.

Then the drums stop. You see the temple walls begin to move as the carvings come to life! They clamber down the walls and stand before you, their red eyes blazing.

To get out of there and wait for the Spook Truck and more weapons, go to 35.

To wait and see what happens next, go to 22.

To attack the figures, go to 13.

You plunge into the water and begin swimming to the opposite bank. Suddenly you see movement in the water ahead of you.

"NOOOO!" you cry as a set of huge jaws explodes from the water and opens up in front of you. It's a mugger crocodile! The creature snaps at you as you desperately try to reach for your BAM gun and stay afloat.

The jaws open again and slam shut on your arm! The water turns red as the crocodile attacks again, sending you to oblivion.

You've been totally mugged! Go back to 1.

48

You head away from the exit and towards one of the minarets. Your plan works as the demon monkeys follow you.

Ahead of you is a snake charmer, holding a flute and crouching against a wall. "Get away!" you warn. "There are incoming monkeys!"

Instead of taking your advice, the charmer puts his flute to his lips and begins to play.

A high-pitched sound fills the air, causing the monkeys to stop their pursuit.

You are amazed as the creatures stand transfixed by the sound.

The snake charmer continues to play and the monkeys begin to transform back into their original form and scamper away.

You turn to the charmer and he takes off his turban. "Hello, Agent!"

You are gobsmacked. It's Cranberry!

Go to 10.

49

You turn and are amazed as the abandoned village begins to shimmer and glow. The light pulses as the ruined huts transform into an ornate white marble palace.

Statues of warriors line the walls and you hear the sound of music coming from inside the palace.

Cautiously, you move towards the palace entrance, but as you do, you see a movement to your right. The statues are moving!

Within seconds they are fully changed into fearsome warriors all holding deadly looking talwar swords.

To attack the warriors, go to 11.
To get out of there immediately, go to 37.

50

Cranberry stands next to the Spook Truck.

"You took your time," you say.

"I got here as soon as I could. Did anything interesting happen in the meantime?"

"You could say that," you reply and tell him what happened. "And I bought you a small souvenir." You throw him the amber amulet you picked up. "It's got symbols scratched into it. Could be interesting..."

Cranberry looks at them. "I'll run them through the G.H.O.S.T. translator." He does so.

"So are they the words of a powerful spell, or the key to a fabulous treasure?" you ask.

"No, Agent," laughs Cranberry. "It says, 'Made in China'!"

You smile. "Things are not always what they appear to be! Let's go home..."

Phantom Flyer: For fast international and intercontinental travel, you use the Phantom Flyer, a supersonic business jet crammed full of detection and communication equipment and weaponry.

Spook Trucks: For more local travel you use one of G.H.O.S.T.'s fleet of Spook Trucks — heavily armed and armoured SUVs you requisition from local agents.

BAM (Blasts All Monsters)

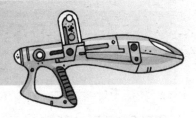

TAME (Transforms All Monsters Easily)

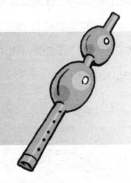

Flame pistol — demons don't like fire!

Drone

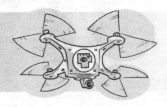

I HERO
MONSTER HUNTER
YETI
EDGE
STEVE BARLOW STEVE SKIDMORE
Illustrated by PAUL DAVIDSON

You are on a G.H.O.S.T. training exercise in the Arctic circle. You are driving a snowmobile across the ice heading for a rendezvous point with a local Inuit agent.

The going is tough as the frozen sea ice is uneven and the wind whips up the snow, making visibility almost impossible.

Suddenly the ice in front of you cracks and splits apart. There is no time to avoid it and you are thrown from the snowmobile onto the ice. The vehicle falls into the crevasse and with it all your survival gear and weapons!

You hear a growl and peering through the swirling ice, you make out the outline of a giant polar bear heading your way. You know if you activate your distress signal, you will fail the training exercise, but the bear is fast approaching and you need a weapon ...

Continue the adventure in:

MONSTER HUNTER
YETI

About the 2Steves

"The 2Steves" are one
of Britain's most popular
writing double acts for
young people, specialising
in comedy and adventure.

Together they have written many books, including the
I HERO Immortals series.

Find out what they've been up to at:
www.the2steves.net

About the illustrator:
Paul Davidson

Paul Davidson is a British
illustrator and comic book artist.

Have you completed these I HERO adventures?

I HERO Immortals — more to enjoy!

Dinosaur Hunter
978 1 4451 6963 7 pb
978 1 4451 6964 4 ebook

Fairy
978 1 4451 6969 9 pb
978 1 4451 6971 2 ebook

Knight
978 1 4451 6957 6 pb
978 1 4451 6959 0 ebook

Pirate Queen
978 1 4451 6954 5 pb
978 1 4451 6955 2 ebook

Samurai
978 1 4451 6960 6 pb
978 1 4451 6962 0 ebook

Witch
978 1 4451 6966 8 pb
978 1 4451 6967 5 ebook

Defeat all the baddies in Toons:

978 1 4451 5930 0 pb
978 1 4451 5931 7 ebook

978 1 4451 5921 8 pb
978 1 4451 5922 5 ebook

978 1 4451 5924 9 pb
978 1 4451 5925 6 ebook

978 1 4451 5918 8 pb
978 1 4451 5919 5 ebook

Also by the 2Steves...

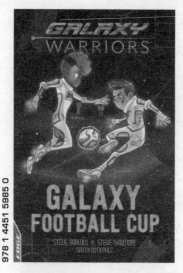

978 1 4451 5985 0

Tip can't believe his luck when he mysteriously wins tickets to see his favourite team in the cup final. But there's a surprise in store ...

978 1 4451 5892 1

Big baddie Mr Butt Hedd is in hot pursuit of the space cadets and has tracked them down for Lord Evil. But can Jet, Tip and Boo Hoo find a way to escape in a cunning disguise?

978 1 4451 5988 1

Jet and Tip get a new command from Master Control to intercept some precious cargo. It's time to become space pirates!

978 1 4451 5979 9

The goodies intercept a distress signal and race to the rescue. Then some eight-legged fiends appear ... Tip and Jet realise it's a trap!